WHO WILL IT BE?

SIMON SPOTLIGHT

An imprint of Simon & Schuster Children's Publishing Division • New York London Toronto Sydney New Delhi
1230 Avenue of the Americas, New York, New York 10020 • This Simon Spotlight edition January 2020
Text by May Nakamura • TM & © 2020 PocketWatch, Inc. & Hour Hand Productions, LLC. All Rights Reserved. Ryan's Mystery Playdate and all related titles, logos, and
characters, and the pocket.watch logo, are trademarks of PocketWatch, Inc. All other rights are the property of their respective owners. • Stock photos by iStock
All rights reserved, including the right of reproduction in whole or in part in any form. • SIMON SPOTLIGHT and colophon are registered trademarks of Simon & Schuster, Inc.
For more information about special discounts for bulk purchases, please contact Simon & Schuster Special Sales at 1-866-506-1949 or business@simonandschuster.com.
Manufactured in the United States of America 0620 CWM
2 4 6 8 10 9 7 5 3
ISBN 978-1-5344-6240-3

Great, we've completed the first challenge. And look what's at the bottom of the slime pool: **our first hint!** *Use your decoder to reveal the hint.*

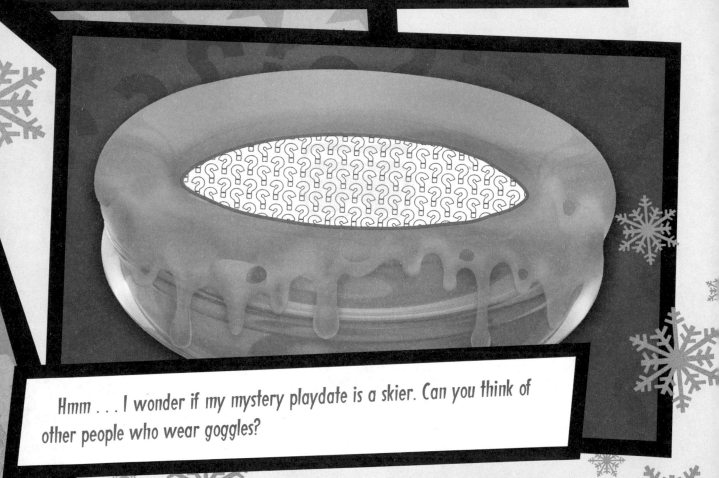

Hmm . . . I wonder if my mystery playdate is a skier. Can you think of other people who wear goggles?

I think we're going to need more hints to figure out who my mystery playdate is.

We discovered what was inside the boxes and solved the challenge! The Mystery Splasher will give us our second hint. *Use your decoder to reveal the hint.*

So many people wear coats, including doctors, dentists, painters, and chefs. Whoever my playdate is, it's still a mystery. Are you ready to earn one more hint? I sure am!

Wow, look at this: it's a mystery box shaped like a rocket! How cool is that? Maybe if we open up the box, we can get our third hint.

Will you help me? First try knocking on the box three times.

Knock, knock, knock!

Then pick up the book and shake it up and down, like the rocket is about to take off.

Shake, shake, shake!

There are more than one hundred billion stars in the Milky Way galaxy!

Great! We've unboxed the third hint. *Use your decoder to reveal the hint.*

It's a little beaker. Have you ever used one before?
A beaker is a cup that some people use to measure liquids.

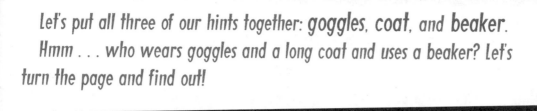

Let's put all three of our hints together: **goggles**, **coat**, and **beaker**. Hmm . . . who wears goggles and a long coat and uses a beaker? Let's turn the page and find out!

My mystery playdate is . . . **a scientist!** Her name is Kate.

Scientists do a lot of cool experiments to figure out why things are the way they are. Different kinds of scientists study subjects like the Earth, the human body, space, technology, and so much more.

My mommy is a scientist too. She used to be a high school science teacher, so she knows a lot of fun science facts.

Some plants, like Venus flytraps, are carnivorous. That means they eat

Babies have more  in their bodies than adults do!

An astronaut's space suit weighs about  pounds on Earth.

For our playdate, Kate and I are having a scientific bubble party.

We dip straws into a mixture of sugar water and dish soap. Then we blow into our straws to make bubbles.

I even made a bubble **inside** a bubble. Wow!

You can join our bubble playdate too. *Use the decoder to make bubbles appear on the page.*

Do you know why bubbles have rainbow-colored swirls? That's because they have water on their surfaces. When light bounces off the water, it makes the bubbles look shimmery and colorful!

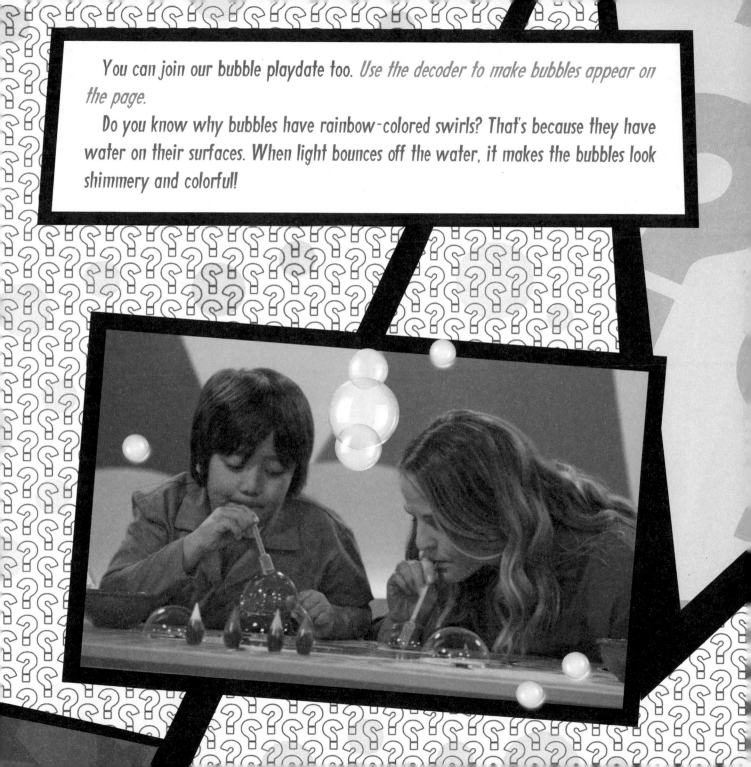

ANSWER KEY

Page 3

Page 4

Page 5

Page 6

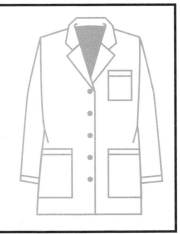

Page 8

Page 11

meat.

bones

280

Pages 12-13